A Feiwel and Friends Book
An imprint of Macmillan Publishing Group, LLC
175 Fifth Avenue, New York, NY 10010

Our books may be purchased in bulk for promotional, educational, or business use. Please contact your local
bookseller or the Macmillan Corporate and Premium Sales Department at (800) 221-7945 ext. 5442 or by email at
MacmillanSpecialMarkets@macmillan.com.

Library of Congress Cataloging-in-Publication Data is available.
ISBN 978-1-250-14567-3

Feiwel and Friends logo designed by Filomena Tuosto
Originally published under the title 나무처럼 in Korea in 2016 by DreamingKite Corp.
First American edition, 2019
1 3 5 7 9 10 8 6 4 2
mackids.com

The
Happiest Tree
A Story of Growing Up

Hyeon-Ju Lee

Feiwel and Friends
New York

I moved to this building when I was ten years old.

Beautiful sounds from the Rose piano class
always filled the ground floor.

The music came to me through the window. I listened to it with my friends, the birds and cats.

I grew up fast. When I turned fourteen years old,
I met Mr. Artist on the second floor.

For the first time ever, I could see myself. I was happy and excited and full of life.

Sometimes, the groundskeeper
trimmed my branches. It was
painful but it helped so that I could
grow up quickly!

When I turned seventeen years old, I could reach the third floor. I was able to glimpse inside the apartment where the Kong family lived.

Mr. Kong was the
father of five puppies.

My times with the Kong family
were some of the happiest of my life.

When I was twenty years old, all that
I could see through the dark fourth-floor
window was a lonely grandmother. She
was sitting in a chair, looking at family
photographs. And I felt . . .

I felt sadness when I looked
at the grandmother.

At twenty-five years old, I had grown to the top floor of the building. However, only my long shadow was beside me.

I was left alone for a long time.

How tall would I be? I spent my
days thinking about things like this.

One day when morning broke,
I stretched my branches above the
rooftop of the building.

Now, I can hear the greetings of other
trees beyond the old building.
I am the happiest ginkgo tree in my town.